What Is in the Box?

written by Lucy McClymont
illustrated by Lindy Burnett

HARCOURT BRACE & COMPANY
Orlando Atlanta Austin Boston San Francisco Chicago Dallas New York
Toronto London

What is in the box?

I see two little ears.

I see two little eyes.

I see a little nose.

I see a little tail.
Is it a very big mouse?

No, it's not a mouse.
Look in the box. You'll see.

It's a little dog!
I wanted one so much!